Brer Bear's Bad Memory

Brer Bear has a bad memory. One day Brer Rabbit shows Brer Bear how to remember things, but Brer Bear is not sure if he should trust him.

Enid Blyton's

Brer Bear's Bad Memory

illustrated by Edgar Hodges

Published in Great Britain by World International Publishing Limited,
An Egmont Company,
Egmont House, P.O.Box 111 Great Ducie Street, Manchester M60 3BL.
Printed in DDR. ISBN 0 7235 4448 4

A CIP catalogue record for this book is available from the British Library.

Brer Bear had a bad memory. He forgot things a hundred times a week, and sometimes it was very awkward.

One day he invited Brer Wolf and Brer Fox
to tea the next day – but he had forgotten the
invitation when the time came, and he went off
to pay a call on his old aunt. So when Brer Fox
and Brer Wolf turned up, expecting a most
delicious tea, they found Brer Bear's house shut
and nobody in at all.

They were angry with Brer Bear, and he was most upset. He sat in his front garden looking very miserable that evening when Brer Rabbit happened along.

"What's up, Brer Bear?" asked Brer Rabbit. So Brer Bear told him.

"If only I could think of something that would remind me to remember things," said Brer Bear.

"Well, why don't you tie a knot in your handkerchief every time you want to remember something?" asked Brer Rabbit. He took out his own yellow handkerchief and showed it to Brer Bear. It had a knot in it. "Look," said Brer Rabbit, pointing to the knot. "That's to remind me to buy some carrots on my way home."

"What a very, very good idea!" said Brer Bear, delighted. "I'll do the same! You just come along tomorrow, Brer Rabbit, and you'll see how well I am remembering everything!"

So the next morning Brer Rabbit ambled
along, and there was Brer Bear in his house,
looking at a knot in his handkerchief with a
very long face.

"Brer Rabbit, this knot business is not going
to work," he said dolefully. "Now I can't
remember what I put the knot there for!"

Brer Rabbit put up his hand and hid a grin.
"Why, Brer Bear," he said, "I can tell you! You
kindly asked me to dinner today!"

Brer Bear looked surprised – and well he
might, for he certainly hadn't asked Brer Rabbit
to dinner. But as his memory was so bad he
thought Brer Rabbit was right, and he set to
work to prepare a tasty dinner.

Brer Rabbit enjoyed it very much. He thanked Brer Bear and skipped home, grinning to think how Brer Bear was so easily tricked!

The next day along went Brer Rabbit again. Once more Brer Bear was looking at his handkerchief in dismay, wondering what he had tied the knot there for.

"I simply can't remember, Brer Rabbit!" he said. "Now what *did* I tie that knot there for?"

"To remind you to give me one of your jars of new honey!" said Brer Rabbit at once. Brer Bear stared at him in surprise and scratched his head. But no amount of scratching could make him remember that he had promised Brer Rabbit some honey. Still, he liked to keep his promises, so he got down a jar and gave it to Brer Rabbit.

"All the same," said Brer Bear, "I'm *not* going to tie knots in my handkerchief any more, Brer Rabbit. It's just no use at all."

Well, Brer Bear untied the knot, and that
night, although he wanted to remember a lot of
things the next day, he didn't tie any knots in
his hanky at all. He just put it on the window-sill
and left it there.

Now Brer Rabbit hopped along that night and spied the handkerchief on the sill. He took it up and put two knots in it. Then he grinned and hopped off.

When he came along the next day he found poor Brer Bear in a state, with the handkerchief on the table in front of him.

"Oh, Brer Rabbit," said Brer Bear, "this is worse than ever! I don't even remember putting knots in my handkerchief – as well as not remembering what I tied them for!"

"Dear, dear!" spoke up Brer Rabbit with a grin. "It's a good thing I'm always able to help you, Brer Bear. You put *that* knot in to remind you to shake your fist at Brer Wolf when he comes by – and you put *that* one in to remind you to buy some lettuces from me today."

"Did I really?" said Brer Bear, astonished. "Brer Rabbit, my memory is getting worse and worse each day!"

"Well, here are the lettuces you said you wanted," said Brer Rabbit, putting three down on the table. "Sixpence, please, Brer Bear."

Brer Bear paid out sixpence and looked at the lettuces in a puzzled way. He didn't like lettuces. Then why did he say he would buy some? He couldn't make it out.

"Look, here comes Brer Wolf!" said Brer Rabbit. "That's the second knot in your hanky, Brer Bear. Shake your fist at him!"

So poor Brer Bear went to the window and shook his fist at Brer Wolf when he went by. Brer Wolf was most amazed, and could hardly believe his eyes. But he was in a hurry, so didn't say anything about it.

Again that night Brer Rabbit slipped along and put a knot into Brer Bear's hanky. In the morning he arrived at Brer Bear's as usual, and saw the knotted handkerchief sticking out of Brer Bear's pocket.

"Hey, Brer Bear!" he cried. "Have you remembered what that knot is for this time?"

"Just take a look at this, Brer Rabbit," said Brer Bear, in an angry voice, and he stuck a piece of paper under Brer Rabbit's nose. On it was written in large letters:

I HAVE NOT PUT ANY KNOTS IN
MY HANKY TONIGHT.
(Signed) BRER BEAR

"Do you see that?" said Brer Bear. "Well, I wrote that last night before I went off to sleep, Brer Rabbit. And yet there's a knot in my hanky this morning. I think perhaps *you* know something about that, don't you?"

Brer Rabbit grinned. "Well maybe I can tell you what it's there for," he said.

"Yes – you'll tell me I asked you to tea, or something like that!" said Brer Bear. "But, Brer Rabbit, I know better this time. That knot's there to remind me to shake you till your teeth rattle in your head! Yes – that's what that knot is for!"

But Brer Rabbit didn't wait for Brer Bear to obey the knot! He quickly scampered off, *lippitty-clippitty*, laughing to think how he had tricked poor old Brer Bear.

As for Brer Bear, he never tied another knot in his handkerchief, and he kept such a close watch for Brer Rabbit that that scamp didn't dare go near him for weeks and weeks!